TRUE ADVENTURES WITH T

Jimmy Martin
Photograph by Jim Herrington

TRUE ADVENTURES WITH THE KING OF BLUEGRASS

Tom Piazza

▼

Foreword by Marty Stuart

THE COUNTRY MUSIC FOUNDATION PRESS

&

VANDERBILT UNIVERSITY PRESS

Nashville

© 1999 by Tom Piazza
Published by Vanderbilt University Press
in cooperation with the
Country Music Foundation Press

This book is printed on acid-free paper made from
50% post-consumer recycled content.
Manufactured in the United States of America

Library of Congress Cataloging-in-Publication Data

Piazza, Tom, 1955–
True adventures with the King of Bluegrass / Tom Piazza ;
foreword by Marty Stuart. —1st ed.
p. cm.
Discography: p.
ISBN 978-0-8265-1680-0 (pbk: alk. paper)
ISBN 0-8265-1360-3 (cloth: alk. paper)
1. Martin, Jimmy. 2. Bluegrass musicians—United States
Biography. I. Title.
ML420.M3318P5 1999
782.421642'092—dc21
[B]   99-6762

"True Adventures with the King of Bluegrass"
originally appeared in *The Oxford American*.

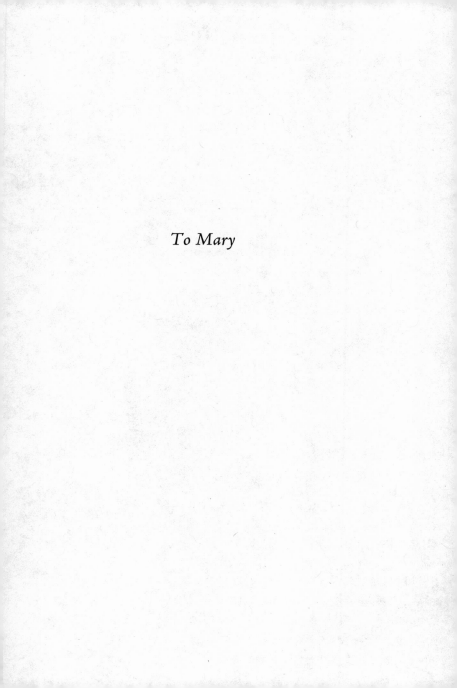

To Mary

Other Books by Tom Piazza

Fiction

City of Refuge
My Cold War
Blues and Trouble

Nonfiction

True Adventures with the King of Bluegrass
Why New Orleans Matters
Blues Up and Down: Jazz in Our Time
Understanding Jazz
The Guide to Classic Recorded Jazz
Setting the Tempo (editor)

Contents

Foreword

Somewhere along the way, moonshine and dynamite collided. The result is the musical genius and three-chord scholar named Jimmy Martin. Baptized in the same fire that gave us Little Richard and Jerry Lee Lewis, this reigning King of Bluegrass is no doubt a charter member of the elite fraternity of Southern musicians that helped forge what the world now knows as bluegrass, rockabilly, country, and rock & roll music.

Jimmy Martin has been spilling his soul into microphones since the late 1940s. Every note of music he's ever recorded melts into a body of work that can be viewed as no less than a masterpiece.

He's part preacher, part prophet, and a card-carrying madman who is completely filled with the musical holy ghost. Time spent with the King of Bluegrass is not for the lily-livered or the faint of heart. It's more than a casual stroll through bongo land. One should expect a cosmic mountain ride throughout the kingdoms of music, coon hunting, love, heartbreak, liquor, dead batteries, more liquor, bright lights, dark valleys, two-tone shoes, heaven, hell, the mild side, the wild side, terror, tone, and timing. It's all somewhere in the neighborhood of B-natural. It's a place where everybody has 20/20 vision, but they're walking around blind.

Check it out.

Marty Stuart
Nashville

Acknowledgments

From the beginning, this piece, and the book that has grown out of it, has had a life of its own. Many people have contributed to it, in many ways. First and foremost, thanks are due to everyone at the *Oxford American*, where "True Adventures" first appeared, especially to its editor, Marc Smirnoff, who sent me to Nashville strictly on faith and then published my piece in full.

People in Nashville could not have been nicer before, during, and after the visit described in "True Adventures." John Hartford was a continual source of stories and encouragement, a great friend in all ways. The same goes for Ellen Pryor. Thanks also to Ernie Sykes and to the staff of the Grand Ole Opry.

Kyle Young was responsible for making a home for this book at the Country Music Foundation. Many thanks, too, to Paul Kingsbury for his patience, flexibility, and care with the various stages of this project and to Chris Dickinson for her fine editing eye. Thanks as well to Charles Backus, Polly

Rembert, and the staff of Vanderbilt University Press and to Jim Herrington for the great photos, John Rumble for the time line, and Marty Stuart for the foreword.

Many thanks to Jeff Rosen for playing me the first Jimmy Martin record I ever heard, to Al Murphy for the tape, and to Peter Guralnick, Eddie Gorodetsky, Stu Bernstein, Dirk Powell, Barry Ancelet, and my mother and father for all the encouragement. Ed Newman made some extremely helpful reader's comments during the early stages of the piece. Thanks to Marianne Merola at Brandt & Brandt, to Kevin Rabalais, my assistant, for invaluable help, repeatedly, in the nick of time, and to Mary Howell for being herself.

Last but not least, thanks to Jimmy Martin, the one and only.

TRUE ADVENTURES WITH THE KING OF BLUEGRASS

It's pitch-dark and cold and I'm sitting in my car at the top of a driveway on a small hill outside Nashville, trying to decide what to do. In an hour and a half, the Grand Ole Opry starts, and I'm supposed to attend with the King of Bluegrass himself—or, rather, the King-In-Exile, the 69-year-old Black Sheep of the Great Dysfunctional Family of Country Music—Jimmy Martin, veteran of Bill Monroe's early-1950s Blue Grass Boys and one-time Decca recording star in his own right. Inside the nearby house, which is totally dark, Jimmy Martin is submerged in some advanced state of inebriation, waiting for me. Outside my car, two of Martin's hunting dogs are howling their heads off in the cold black night air in a frenzy of bloodlust.

I've hit the horn a few times, but no lights have gone on, no doors have opened. The Dodge van and the Ford pickup are there, with the coon-hunting bumper stickers (WHEN THE TAILGATE DROPS, THE BULLSHIT STOPS), as is the midnight-blue 1985 Lincoln stretch limousine in which we took his garbage to the town incinerator yesterday, so I know he didn't run out on me. Finally, I tentatively open my door to see if I can make it to the house, but one of the dogs comes peeling around the front bumper and I close it again, fast. I decide to pull out and call him from the gas station on the corner of Old Hickory Boulevard.

It's kind of beautiful out here, actually. Hermitage is an eastern suburb of Nashville about fifteen minutes out Interstate 40 from downtown. Rolling hills, shopping centers, subdivisions, plus the usual swelling of motels and fast-food joints around the highway interchange, like an infection around a puncture wound. The main attraction is President Andrew Jackson's house, the Hermitage, where historically minded Nashville tourists can go for a couple hours' respite from the Eternal Twang.

I have always wanted to meet Jimmy Martin. I heard that he was a difficult person, but I don't know if anything could have prepared me for the last two days. But you may not even know who Jimmy Martin is, so first things first. . . .

One night in 1949, a completely unknown 22-year-old singer-guitarist from Sneedville, Tennessee, walked up to Bill Monroe backstage at the Grand Ole Opry and asked if he could sing him a song. Monroe agreed, and before an hour had passed he invited the young man on the road with his band, the Blue Grass Boys. At that time, Monroe and his mandolin had already pioneered the sound that would become known as bluegrass, a form of country music reaching back to earlier mountain styles and adding an emphasis on instrumental precision and virtuosity. Monroe's two most-famous sidemen of the 1940s, the guitarist-singer Lester Flatt and the banjoist Earl Scruggs, were as important in many ways to the music's development as Monroe; when they left the Blue Grass Boys, in 1948, they were stars in their own right.

Martin's arrival brought another element into the group; his high, strong voice, stronger than Lester Flatt's, gave a new edge to the vocal blend, and his aggressive guitar added a stronger push to the rhythm as well. His early-1950s recordings with Monroe, including "Uncle Pen," "River of Death," and "The Little Girl and the Dreadful Snake," are classics. After five years with Monroe, Martin went on his own, first teaming up with the very young Osborne Brothers and then forming his own group. The 1957–1961 incarnation of the Sunny Mountain Boys, as he called them, with the mandolinist Paul Williams and the banjo prodigy J. D. Crowe, is widely regarded as one of the greatest bands in bluegrass history.

Martin had a string of hits in the late 1950s and early 1960s, including "Ocean of Diamonds," "Sophronie," the truck-driving anthem "Widow Maker," "You Don't Know My

Mind," and his signature tune, "Sunny Side of the Mountain." Martin's vocals—high, plaintive, and lonesome—wrung every bit of meaning and feeling out of the lyrics. Like many country performers, he was capable of astonishing sentimentality, musical crocodile tears, like his duet with his young daughter on "Daddy, Will Santa Claus Ever Have To Die?" But at his best his phrasing, the impact of the urgency behind his long, held notes, could be staggering.

Although his early recordings are considered bluegrass classics, to my ears he seemed to take more chances and gain in expressiveness as he got older. In 1973 he received a gold record, along with Roy Acuff, Doc Watson, Merle Travis, and Maybelle Carter, for his contribution to the Nitty Gritty Dirt Band's first *Will The Circle Be Unbroken* album; his performances are arguably the best thing about that record.

Despite all this, Martin has remained a kind of shadowy figure, with much less of a public profile than some of his bluegrass peers, like Ralph Stanley or the Osborne Brothers. He is seen in Rachel Liebling's excellent 1991 bluegrass documentary film *High Lonesome*, but the glimpses are only tantalizing. In some ways Martin doesn't fit into the categories that have evolved in the country music world. He is too raw for the commercial and slick Nashville establishment and in a way too unapologetically country in the old sense—mixing sentiment and showmanship with George Jones— and Hank Williams— style barroom heartbreak—for the folk revival types to whom bluegrass was, and is, essentially folk music. On top of that, the King of Bluegrass, as he called himself, had a reputation as a heavy drinker and a volatile personality. As I asked around, I began to realize that Nashville insiders traded Martin stories back and forth the way 1960s Washington insiders used to tell Lyndon Johnson stories.

Still, his obscurity was hard for me to fathom. When I got into bluegrass, after 25 years of listening to jazz, Martin seemed, and still seems, to be the greatest. On heartbreak songs he could tell it like it is, with no posing, only pure truth.

> Tomorrow's just another day to worry.
> To wake up, my dear, and I wonder why
> Must a sea of heartache slowly drown me?
> Why can't I steal away somewhere and die?

He sang to the hilt, as if the full weight of a human life hung on every line. His phrasing was alive with expressive turns, his voice breaking at times, or falling off a note he had held just long enough. His nasal, reedy tones reached back all the way to country music's deepest Scotch-Irish roots; at its highest and lonesomest, his voice conveyed the near-madness and absolutism of bagpipes in full cry. The only comparison in my experience was to the keening sound of certain jazz players, the altoist Jackie McLean or, especially, the tenor giant John Coltrane. Why, I always wondered, wasn't he everybody's favorite?

I did some digging and got his phone number and in early October of last year called to try and set up an interview. From the first he was guarded, suspicious, and it was clear that he was in no rush to have me visit. His voice was unmistakable from his records—high, nasal, and deep country—and he spoke loud and in italics much of the time. After some confusion over my name (*"Tom T. Hall?"*), he gave a series of grunted, grudging responses to my initial comments about why I was calling. When I told him he was my favorite bluegrass singer he shifted gears a little, thanking me and saying, "I can't *tell* you how many thousands of people have told me that over the years. When did you want to come up and see me?" I suggested a date in November, and he began hedging, saying that he would be spending a lot of time out of town coon hunting. We agreed that I'd call him in a week or two to see how his plans were shaping up.

A week and a half later I called him again to try and zero in on a date. It was immediately obvious not only that he didn't remember our previous conversation ("Tom T. *WHAT?*"), but that he was drunk. I started explaining that I wanted to write a piece on him, but he cut me off in mid-sentence.

"*Whut . . .* ," he began, dramatically, "is *in* this . . ." another dramatic pause, "for *Jimmy Martin?*" His speech was heavy and over-deliberate, rather than slurred.

Before I could answer, he broke in and said, "Publicity?"

"Well, yeah . . . ," I began.

"I mean," he said, "what kind . . . of money . . . is in it?"

"Well," I began, again, realizing that he probably hadn't had a lot of magazine articles done on him lately, "magazines don't really do that. They don't pay the subjects of . . ." —and here he broke in again—

"*You're . . .* ," he said, "telling *me . . .* what *magazines* do?"

Uh-oh, I thought.

"I've had *all kinds* of write-ups," he went on, cranking up, his voice suddenly seething with a weirdly intimate rage. "I'm the *KING OF BLUEGRASS*, and *you're . . .* telling *me . . .* what *magazines* do?"

I wasn't sure what I was supposed to say to this, so I kept quiet.

"I'm just saying," he went on, picking up a little speed now, as if there were a response expected of me that he could see I was going to be too dim to get, so he was going to have to lob me the serve one more time, "is there gonna be a *few dollars* in it for Jimmy Martin to buy himself a *fifth* of *whiskey?*"

This, I began to sense, was some kind of test. Feeling my way, I said, "I tell you what . . . if you want to do the interview . . . I'll bring you the fifth of whiskey *myself.*"

"*ALL*-right," he hollered, sounding hugely pleased. "*COME 'n see me.* When you wanna come up?"

I suggested a date in mid-November, and he said it would be fine. Then he said, "Listen . . . I gotta go. I got a black girl here tryin' to talk to me. You know what . . . every white girl I ever went with, she got a *home* offa me. Now I'm gonna see about a *black* one and tell the others to *kiss my ass.* How does *that* sound to you?"

I said it made sense, and he said, "Good. Call me closer to the time," then he hung up and I sat at my desk, shaking my head. After that call I had a pang of misgiving about the whole idea, as if I might be getting myself into something I'd prefer to stay out of, but I was too curious to give up. Boy, I thought. Whatever you do, don't forget that whiskey.

Over the next month we talked two more times. The first time, he sounded sober and friendly, even asking me one or two questions about myself. He had a happy memory of New Orleans, where I live ("I played down there when Johnny Horton had his hit on 'Battle of New Orleans.' We played 'Ocean of Diamonds' and 'Sophronie' and tore his ass to pieces"), and we were able to set a date of November 20, a Wednesday, for me to come up, but there was only one hitch. What I had to do, he said, was call the weather report for Richmond, Indiana, that week and see what the temperature was going to be. If it was going to be in the thirties up there, it would be too cold to go coon hunting and I could come see him in Nashville. But if it was going to be in the forties or fifties, then I might as well stay home because he'd be in Indiana, hunting. I had no intention of calling the weather report in Indiana; I decided to just call Martin again a few days beforehand.

On November 17, the Sunday before I was to go up, I called him to confirm, and he was the old Jimmy again; he grumbled, chafed ("Now, that's *how* many days you're taking up?"), but I finally got him to agree that I would drive up on Wednesday, we would visit on Thursday, and then we could take it from there. Thursday, right? Yep. Okay. See you then. Hang up.

That's it. I was going.

à à à

Photograph by Jim Herrington

The drive from New Orleans took ten hours. As soon as I arrived at the Holiday Inn in Hermitage that Wednesday night, I called Martin.

"Oh, hell," he said, gloomily. "I was fixing to spend tomorrow rabbit hunting. But I guess I'll spend it with you. . . ." He sounded like a teenager forced to bring his kid brother along on a date. We agreed that I'd come over at ten in the morning; he gave me directions to his house, and that was it.

Thursday dawned grey and raw; yellow leaves blew around the motel parking lot. I had breakfast and ran through some of the things I wanted to ask Martin, but I was already realizing that the questions I wanted to ask him weren't really the point of this trip. Whatever I was looking for I probably wouldn't find by asking him a bunch of questions. But it was a place to start, at least.

His house, it turned out, was closer than I realized, and five minutes before ten A.M. I pulled up to the big iron gates he had described, at the foot of a long blacktop driveway leading up to a large, ochre-colored ranch house on several hilly acres of land. At the top of the driveway I could see a figure moving. I made my way up the driveway and parked in some mud off to the right, the only paved spots being taken up by a couple of vans and a long, midnight-blue stretch limousine, the rear license plate of which read KING JM. Across the lip of the limo's trunk, yellow and orange letters spelled out the title of his best-known hit: SUNNY SIDE OF THE MOUNTAIN. The moving figure was, of course, Martin, attended by two dogs that bayed lustily at my approach. Martin didn't stop what he was doing or register my arrival in any way; by the time I opened the door of my car he had disappeared into the limo, and as I got out his taillights squeezed bright and the limo started to back up.

I grabbed my stuff and approached the limo, the tinted driver's-side window rolled down halfway, and there was Jimmy Martin looking up at me, unsmiling, suspicion in his

Photograph by Jim Herrington

red and slightly watery eyes, his head as big as a large ham and very jowlly, with long grey sideburns and thin grey hair combed straight back and left a little bit long by the collar of his black nylon windbreaker.

"Leave your bags in your car," he said. "I gotta do an errand here; you can come with me."

By the time I climbed into his passenger seat, Martin was trying to maneuver the limo into a five-point U-turn so that he could get it out of his driveway. He worked the gear shift, which was on the steering column, with dogged concentration and without saying a word. The hood was as big as a queen-sized bed. On the first leg of the turn the limo stalled, and Martin cursed and restarted it with effort. The car stalled twice more before he got it through the turn; at one point he spun the wheels and they splattered mud all over my car, which was about twenty feet behind the limo. Finally, the turn was completed and we coasted down the driveway with the engine gurgling uncertainly, and out onto the road.

Once we were underway I tried a few conversation openers, but it was like trying to play tennis in the sand. It took three long minutes, driving at about 15 miles an hour, to get to our destination just off the main road: the back of a one-story brick building where somebody was busy throwing wood and other garbage into an incinerator.

"Wait here," Martin said, getting out and slamming the door. For the first time I turned and looked in the back area of the limo, which was upholstered in blue velvet but not very well cared for, littered with scraps of paper and junk. In the middle of the back seat were two giant bags of garbage and a broken crutch. Martin opened the back door, grabbed the garbage, and closed it again. I watched him bring it over to the guy; they stood around talking, inaudibly to me, for about five minutes while I sat in the front seat.

When they were finished Martin got back in without any explanation, and we headed back to the house, with the limo stalling only once more.

The dogs were really whooping it up when we arrived, and Martin hollered at them as we got out and they skulked away quietly. At the end of the driveway stood a big STOP sign, with stick-on letters added, reading BAD DOG WILL BITE TAIL. I grabbed my bags out of my car and followed Martin inside.

We walked under a carport and through a storm door into an unheated den, where the floor was piled with boxes of cassettes, CDs, an upright bass, sound equipment, and other stuff. I followed him up a few steps, through a door and past a daybed where a collection of mesh caps of all sorts was displayed, then through another door into a vestibule with a bathroom and a bedroom off of it, which led directly into the kitchen. It was obviously a bachelor's house: clothes were set out to dry on a chair by the heater, and at the Formica kitchen table space would have had to be cleared amid papers, mail-order catalogs, letters, and empty cassette cases to make room for a second person to eat. I unpacked my cassette recorder and notebook while Martin wordlessly looked through some mail, but before we got started I was going to give him the whiskey I had promised him.

I had put some thought into the choice, actually. I had initially bought him a bottle of Knob Creek, a very good Kentucky bourbon. But after I bought it I wondered if there wouldn't be some state loyalty involved in Martin's whiskey preference. He had begun life in Tennessee, after all, and had spent the last 25 years living there. Tennessee was the home of the Grand Ole Opry, etc., etc., and for all I knew some kind of horrible blood rivalry might exist between Tennessee and Kentucky. So I went back to the liquor store and picked up a bottle of Gentleman Jack as well, to cover the Tennessee base.

Now I reminded him of the conversation, made a little speech about my rationale for the choice, during which he looked blankly at the bottles, then I handed the bottles to him, feeling proud of myself.

"I drink Seagram's 7," he said. Then he walked across the kitchen, stashed the bottles in a cabinet, and that was that.

The interview started slowly. We discussed a few things perfunctorily for a while. (Do you have a favorite country singer? "George Jones." Why? "'Cause he's the best.") He also said he liked Hank Williams, Roy Acuff, Ernest Tubb, Bill Monroe, Lester Flatt and Earl Scruggs, and Marty Stuart. His favorite guitarists were Chet Atkins and Doc Watson. Not Merle Travis? I asked. "Well, yeah, I would have to say Merle Travis. Put Merle Travis in there. . . ."

Before long, though, he steered the conversation to what turned out to be his main preoccupation: the fact that he has never been invited to join the Grand Ole Opry. His exclusion clearly causes him pain; he has various theories about why he has been passed by, but he has not given up hope of being asked. He produced letters from a number of people in and out of the music business in which they sang his praises and expressed wonder that he wasn't on it. It is obviously the great frustration of his life. To grasp why, one has to realize that to someone of Martin's generation, who grew up listening to it on the radio, the Opry *was* country music. All the greatest stars were on it; it was the pinnacle of exposure and prestige. Being on the Opry was tantamount to being in a family; being asked to join was the final seal of approval on a performer, an entrance into a pantheon that included all of one's heroes—Hank Williams, Roy Acuff, Bill Monroe, Ernest Tubb, and on and on. Martin has been lobbying for his inclusion for years, and we talked about the question for a good while before I could lead him on to other things.

Once we got past the topic he relaxed a little and actually started to be fun company. He has a good sense of humor, which balances out his tendency to talk about how rough he's had it. He really started to warm up when he talked about hunting. A perfect day, he said, is one on which he can "get my beagle dogs and take 'em out and run 'em and just enjoy their voices." It turns out that he has named most of his hunting dogs after other country singers. "My beagle dogs," he said, "are named George Jones, Earl Scruggs, Little Tater Dickens, and Marty Stuart. My coon dogs are Tom T. Hall, Turbo, Cas Walker, Cas Walker Jr. . . ."

"Turbo?" I said.

"He's named after that motor in them hot rods; we say his voice sounds like Number Five just went by." Martin then did an eerily realistic dog bark—guttural at first, then quickly louder and tapering off, like a loud car passing really fast. "I go out huntin' sometimes with Marty Stuart [referring now to the man, not his canine namesake]. Earl Scruggs just called the other day; he just had a quadruple bypass operation. Little

Jimmy Dickens goes hunting rabbits with me. Ain't nothin' no better than a rabbit fried in a skillet, good and brown, and make gravy in the skillet, then make you some biscuits, then you can just tell Kroger's what to do with their steaks." At this he laughed a beautiful, infectious laugh.

"Country music," he said, "what makes it is you're singing by the way you've had to live. And if you had a hard life to live, then you sing a hard life song. Then you turn around and sing about how good you wish it *could* have been. When I sing, whether it's recording or at a show, or just sittin' down here with you, I give it all I got from the heart. And if it'd be something sad in there, I've *hit* that sad road. 'Cause I used to be barefooted, no shoes on my feet, had no dad when I was four years old, nobody to give me a dollar to go to a show. Had to walk five miles to town to see a show. We'd get one pair of shoes when it frosted, and time it got warmin' up your toes was walkin' out of 'em. You wore 'em day and night and everywhere you went.

"In writin' songs," he went on, "you gotta have something good to write *about*. You can't just sit down and say I'm just absolutely gonna write a song out of nowhere—and that's just about the way the song sounds. It has to *hit* you."

Referring to a recent song he had written, he said, "*That* song started and I'm sittin' on the damn *commode*—all reared back and I start in to write that thing. And I've heard a lot of

Photograph by Jim Herrington

people say that's where it *started*, on the commode. Well, I'll tell you, the best place to read the newspaper, get you a glass and sit on the goddamn commode and read and read and read and enjoy it better'n anything in the world." Again he laughed and laughed at this. He was so out front with everything, and I decided I really liked him, even if he was hard to deal with.

I asked him if he had a favorite time in his life. He thought for a second and said, "I was glad that Bill Monroe hired me, but sometimes that was rough there. Traveling six in a car, with the bass tied on top, used to sleep on each others' shoulders, that was the pillow, worked seven days a week, seven nights. . . . I guess for enjoyment, when I had Paul Williams and J. D. Crowe with me, on the Louisiana Hayride, and in Wheeling, West Virginia. We could really sing it, really pick it; we had it down just right. J. D. Crowe was fourteen years old. I learned him how to sing baritone and how to tone his voice in with mine. Paul, too. We slept in the same house and could rehearse and get it down like we wanted to.

"Seems like that's when I liked to sing, and. . . . We'd ride along in the cars and sing our songs and enjoy it, get it to soundin' good. In those days everybody liked to sing, and liked to hear that harmony, liked to get it better so they could make more money. Playin' in them little bars for five dollars a night and tips. And sayin', 'Oh, God, please help me get good enough to get out of here.' And *mean* that. Now the boys meet me at the festivals backstage, we show up—'Are you in tune?' 'Yeah, let me see if we are'—go on, do the show, and go off. . . . It just ain't as good as it was then. And I hate to say this, but it never *will* be, because it's run different. Most of the bands don't even travel in the same car and come to the shows together. They come with their girlfriends, or their wives, or whatsoever, so it's a girlfriend deal, it's not a professional deal. And it shouldn't be like that; business should be *business*. If you're gonna make a living at it.

"They're payin' big money, though," he said, with a tinge of bitterness audible now. "But there's little rehearsin'. *No* rehearsin', to tell you the truth. My band don't know what it is to rehearse. If they get out there the night before I do, or stay a night after, they might jam out there and play everything in the world, but there's no rehearsin'. Nothin' *serious*. You can't go into a job just laughin' and having fun and expect to show what you're doing. If you're driving a bulldozer you're liable to run over something. You got to have your mind down to the *business*. And I've been told this many times: 'You just take your music too serious.' I don't see how you could be too serious about somethin' that's gonna feed your family and make you a living the rest of your life. I don't see as you could *get* too serious about that." At my expression of surprise, Martin said, "The man who said that couldn't *pick*. A man that don't wanna get serious about somethin', he don't wanna get *good*. Am I right?" He was, of course, right, but the pressure behind the way he said it spoke of some buried frustration, a sense of injustice, of not being sufficiently recognized for his own abilities while standards were falling apart all around him. . . .

As I was thinking this, he looked at me and said, "But the biggest thing I have been asked by the public is 'Why ain't you on the Grand Ole Opry? Why can't we hear you on the Grand Ole Opry?' I just laugh back and I say, 'Well, I guess I just ain't good enough.'"

He showed me a photo of a plaque commemorating his induction into the International Bluegrass Music Association Hall of Honor, which he was very proud of. Then we started to wind down. We had gotten along well, after all, and I liked him. He was opinionated as hell, cranky, and overbearing, but he was honest and had a great sense of gusto for life, and real passion about his music. He was himself, nothing else, and that alone is hard to come by. Still, I felt we had only scratched the surface, and I wanted to see him in some other context if possible, get a feeling for how he related to other people. He said he enjoyed our conversation, and we talked about getting together again later in the weekend, since I was staying in Nashville until Sunday.

At one point I mentioned that I was going to try and get to see the Grand Ole Opry, and he cautioned me to get my ticket quick if I didn't have one already. Then he suggested that we might go together.

"Really?" I said.

Sure, he said, they all knew him backstage, and we could just go inside that way.

I didn't want to scare him off by seeming too excited about the idea, but it was perfect. He asked me to check and see who was going to be on the Opry, which runs on Friday and Saturday nights, and we agreed to talk about it the next day.

On my way out, walking through the den, Martin gave me two of his cassettes out of a couple of big cardboard boxes, and sold me two more at ten dollars apiece. Then he pointed out a selection of mesh caps in various colors, emblazoned with a "Jimmy Martin—King of Bluegrass" logo. I chose one in burgundy with gold lettering, which I thought was a bargain at five dollars. Now I had the rest of the day to look around Nashville.

❧ ❧ ❧

Roughly speaking, Nashville today is at least two towns. First, and best, is downtown, where you can find the old Ryman Auditorium (home of the Grand Ole Opry until its move to suburban Opryland in 1974), the original Ernest Tubb Record Shop (where they used to have the post-Opry broadcasts on Saturday nights after the crowds left the Ryman), Tootsie's Orchid Lounge, and other landmarks. Downtown is the province of the ghosts who make country music something worth thinking about seriously—Hank Williams, Roy Acuff, Lefty Frizzell, and on and on. It attracts the hipper tourists and musicians with a sense of tradition, as well as quite a few aging, struggling characters in denim, Western shirts, and cowboy boots.

Just west of downtown lies Music Row, the heart and soul, if you can call it a soul, of New Nashville, where you find the big music publishers, record companies, ASCAP headquarters, the Country Music Hall of Fame, and gift shops owned by Barbara Mandrell, George Jones, and other luminaries. Music Row can be a little rough on you if you think country music is still about deep, soulful expression from the hills and honky-tonks. The Country Music Hall of Fame, for example, is a lot of fun for anybody with an interest in country music, full of great artifacts and video installations. But most of the Hall of

Fame's visitors waltz past the rare Hank Williams photos and Uncle Dave Macon videos vacant-eyed and clueless, in order to gape at the Reba McEntire and Garth Brooks exhibits. Well, there's nothing wrong with that, but it is a clue to the sensibility of the New Nashville's bread-and-butter constituency.

Music Row contains no shadowy cubbyholes full of interesting stuff, the way old downtown does. The senior citizens who get off of the tour buses in matching warm-up suits don't want shadowy and interesting; they want bright and aggressively heartwarming. They graze happily among the T-shirts and souvenir spoon rests and coffee mugs at Barbara Mandrell's store, where a Christmas-sale sign reads: SPECIAL: NATIVITIES 25% OFF, which just about says it all, and at the George Jones Gift Shop, where rows and rows of glass display shelves under bright fluorescent lights are crammed with frilly dolls, little ceramic figurines, souvenir spoons, salt and pepper shakers, coffee mugs reading "I'm not grouchy—I'm constipated. . . ."

All of which, I thought, helps explain why Jimmy Martin might be anathema to New Nashville. Imagine the souvenir-spoon crowd listening to him sing "Steal Away Somewhere and Die." Not likely. Yet all the garishness and bad taste is no aberration; it's part of the fiber of the world that country music serves. You can't really separate one from the other, any more than you can just forget about Martin performances like "I'd Rather Have America" and "Daddy, Will Santa Claus Ever Have To Die?"

That night I had dinner with a friend, a well-known songwriter and performer who has lived in Nashville for almost thirty years and was part of the so-called New Breed of younger figures who shook up the town in the late 1960s. My friend is actually something of a connoisseur of Jimmy Martin stories, and he added a few to my stockpile, including one about a trip, involving Martin and a couple other musicians, to see Clint Eastwood's movie *Unforgiven*. At one point in the movie a small country shack came on the screen, and Martin supposedly stood up at his seat and hollered, "That shack there is just like the one Jimmy Martin grew up in, back in Sneedville, Tennessee, that y'all been asking me about, folks." Everybody in the theater turned around wondering what the hell was going on, while Martin's companions sank low into their seats.

After we laughed about this, my friend went on, "But, at the same time, I'll never forget once we were having this benefit concert for a local band who had had an accident on the road and needed money. The whole bluegrass community had rallied to their support and held a benefit concert, which Jimmy hadn't been invited to appear on. Late in the evening, though, he showed up backstage anyway, real quiet, with a big jar, like a Mason jar, full of coins and bills. He had had a show earlier that night and he had collected all that money from his audience himself, and he wanted to contribute it. It wasn't a showy thing at all; he just gave it and left quietly.

"Another time," my friend went on, "the son of some dear mutual friends of Jimmy's and mine had died under extremely tragic circumstances, and one of the visitors during the worst of this episode was Jimmy. He walked in and he had obviously been crying beforehand. He had some little plaster statue he had bought for them, maybe it was a Madonna, and as soon as he got in, he just let it all out, crying and saying how sorry he was that it had happened and how much he loved them. . . ." My friend stopped talking for a moment, and I realized he was trying to keep from crying himself. "He only stayed for about five minutes," he went on. "But of all the visits during those days, that's the one that was maybe the most moving."

He kind of shook his head. I could relate; even in the short time I had spent with Martin I could see those disproportions—the deep loneliness and the huge ego, the self-assertion and the sensitivity and the defensiveness. When I mentioned the possibility that I might go to the Opry with Martin, my friend looked at me and raised his eyebrows. "If there's any chance of doing that," he said, "don't miss it. Something interesting will happen."

"I know," I said. "That's what I'm afraid of."

That was last night. Earlier today Martin and I talked on the phone and he said he wanted to go; he told me to get dressed up ("Not like what you come to see me in yesterday") and meet him at his house at 6 o'clock. My first stab at doing that, ten minutes ago, was unsuccessful, and I had to call him from the gas station to get him to let me in. From the sound of his voice he's in no shape to go anywhere, but he insists he wants to go.

Now, as I pull up to his house again, I finally see him, in my headlights, struggling to open the screen door, and I turn my lights and motor off. He's yelling at the dogs, and they quiet down. I get out of the car, but he has already disappeared back into the house. I follow, groping my way through his den in the dark.

The only light on in the house appears to be the overhead one in the kitchen. As I enter the room Martin is sitting down in his chair at the kitchen table. He's wearing his blue jumpsuit, and his eyes are unfocused.

"I'm higher than a Georgia . . . kite," he says. "I know what they'll say. . . . 'Jimmy Martin's been drinkin' again. . . .' But I don't owe them anything." He looks up at me. "Do I?"

I can see his eyes pull into focus. "Where's your Jimmy Martin cap?" he says, squinting at me.

"I left it back at the hotel," I say. His eyes narrow into slits. "I can borrow one of yours," I offer, "if you want me to wear one."

"You got one of your own, didn't you?"

"You said on the phone you wanted me to get a little dressed up, so—"

"So it's fuck Jimmy Martin."

Silence.

"Listen," he says, steadying himself with his forearm on the table. "If I give you the keys to the limo . . . will you drive? Can you drive the limo?"

The *limo?*

"Jimmy," I say, "why don't we just take my car—"

"*NO*," he says, his voice rising. "We're takin' the *limo*, with 'Sunny Side of the Mountain' along the back and everything. They'll recognize it. They *know* me. Can you drive it?"

"Why don't we—"

"*We're takin' the limo*," he says. "We can drive right inside. Whoever says hello says hello." He stands up, unsteadily. "Me

and you are goin' to the Opry," he says. "Did you get you a
drink?" he says.

"No," I say.

"Well go and git you one. Right there."

"Where, Jimmy?"

"*In the cabinet*," he says. I find the cabinet he's indicating,
and inside it the bottle of Knob Creek I gave him yesterday,
with about an inch and a half of bourbon left in it.

"Me and you are goin' to the Opry," he says, shuffling past
me and leaving the room. "Don't drink too much."

I'm standing here and I don't know what to do. I'm almost
overwhelmed by a feeling of not wanting to be here. The single
overhead light, this chaos, the malevolent magnetic field he
generates. I want to get out. But at the same time, it's *Jimmy
Martin. . . .*

Now I hear a grunting sound coming from a small room off
the kitchen. I say, "Are you okay, Jimmy?"

"Come see what I'm doin'."

I walk back to the garage end of the kitchen and look in
the doorway to where he is, and it's his bedroom, small, barely
enough room for the double bed on which Martin is sitting,
utterly transformed. His hair is neat and he is wearing black
slacks, a fire-engine-red shirt buttoned at the neck, and white
leather boots with little multi-colored jewels sewn on.

"Wait a minute, now," he says. He gets a black Western jacket out of the closet and puts it on, then a clip-on tie, white leather with little tassels at the bottom. "All right, hold on," he says, and from a chair in the corner he grabs a white straw cowboy hat with feathers arranged as a hat band.

"How do I look?" he says, now, presenting himself to me. "Huh?"

"You look great," I tell him. I'm not lying. Getting dressed up for these guys is a form of warfare, total plumage warfare, and Martin hasn't been a pro for 48 years for nothing.

It is not quite 6:30 by the time we leave the house. The night outside is cold, cloudless, and moonless. Just outside the carport, the limo is a long, sleek, indistinct presence in the darkness. Opening the driver's door is a small project in itself; the seat is cold through my slacks, and when I pull the door shut it closes like the lid of a tomb. Martin is next to me in the passenger seat.

I turn the ignition and the limo grumbles to life while I fish around for the lights. The rear window, way back there, is about the size and shape of a business envelope, so I lower my window to look out behind. I slide her into reverse, a hard shift, and ease off the brake.

"Cut her back and to the right as hard as you kin," Martin says. "Cut her."

I'm cutting her and hoping I'm not going to hit the tree that I know is back there. When I get what I think is far enough back I shift into drive and it stalls out immediately.

"Oh, boy," Martin says. "Go ahead and start her up again."

I start her, pull her into gear and move forward until the front bumper is almost against the Dodge van's rear bumper, where it stalls again. My own car is sitting halfway under the carport, boxed in now by the limo, and I look at it nostalgically in the headlights. I try to start the limo again; Martin is saying, "Cut the lights! Cut the lights!"

I cut the lights and try again quickly, but it won't even turn over.

"We done it now," Martin says.

I try to get it going another time or two, but the limo is dead. "Son of a bitch," Martin says, opening the passenger door. "Crack the hood."

Martin disappears into the house. I get out and open the gigantic hood; I can hear the dogs moving back and forth somewhere in the darkness. My car is completely blocked in by the dead limousine.

Now Martin reappears; he's carrying something about the size of a shoebox, and trailing a long, heavy-duty orange extension cord. He hands me the plug from the box and the end of the extension cord.

"Plug this in there," he says.

The end of the extension cord seems like it's been melted, and the plug tines won't fit into it easily. I'm struggling with the fit, and I feel it start to slide in when I'm blinded by a bright shower of sparks in my face. I drop the cord and the plug on the ground and stand there trying to get my sight back.

"Which one of these is red?" I hear him asking me. I blink my eyes a few times; he's holding out the charger clamps. I squint, but it's hard to see them; it's too dark. . . .

"Can't you tell which one of these is red?" he says.

I look at him for a second. I breathe slowly through my nose. "Why don't you turn on a light?" I say.

He heads off someplace again, and I try the plug again and get it in this time. Martin comes back and gets the clamps attached, and I go and turn the ignition and it zooms to life. While it is charging, Martin tells me to get the jumper cables out of his Ford pickup and throw them in the back of the limo. He disconnects the clamps and puts the charger away and we get back into the limo, and I maneuver it through its turn, and we head out, slowly, down the driveway and out onto the road. I'm trying to breathe nice and slowly.

"Me and you are goin' to the Grand Ole Opry," he says now. "And your name is *what?*"

"Tom Piazza," I say.

"Tom," he repeats, as if going over a set of difficult instructions. "And you're doin' a article."

"Right."

"Okay."

We pull onto I-40 West, heading toward Nashville. We need to get to Briley Parkway and go north to Opryland. Outside the car, the Tennessee hills pass in the dark like huge, slumbering animals. I'm holding the limo steady right around fifty and most cars are passing me, but that's okay. I'm in no hurry. This is an island of tranquility here. God only knows what's going to happen when we get to the Opry. I know Martin has feuds with various members of the Opry; he's not crazy about the Osborne Brothers, and I've heard that he especially has a problem with Ricky Skaggs, one of the younger generation of bluegrass stars. Evidently Skaggs was a guest on Martin's latest CD and wouldn't sing the tenor part that Martin wanted him to sing because it was too high. Martin feels that Skaggs' refusal was a form of attempted sabotage, motivated by professional jealousy, although Skaggs, of course, is the one with the spot on the Opry.

Now Briley Parkway comes up, with the sign for Opryland, and this is the last definite turn I know; from here on

I have to rely on Martin. I take the exit and follow the curve along to the right.

"Do I look alright?" he asks.

I tell him he looks great.

"When we go down here I want you to be close to me now, and everything," he says.

"I'll be right next to you the whole time," I say.

"Tell 'em who you are."

"Okay."

"You a magazine man—Tom, right?"

"Right."

Now, off to the left, Opryland appears, a city of lights in the darkness. Big tour buses pass us as we make our way along in the right lane; the traffic is much denser now. We go under a bridge, exit, and curl up and back around over Briley Parkway, and there, ahead of us, are the gates to Opryland. I'm happy to be somewhere near civilization. I follow the line of traffic through the entrance. "When's the last time you came to the Opry?" I ask, breathing a little easier now that we've found the place.

"I can come down here anytime I *want* to," he says.

"Yeah," I say, "but when's the last time you did?"

"I'd say it's been about six months," he says. "But they'll

know me well enough. They'll know me. Just walk in there with me. Your name's what?"

We're being funneled into Opryland, with giant tour buses looming outside the windows like ocean liners over a rowboat. "Boy, ain't that got it?" he says. Out the front windshield, spread all out before us, is a huge jungle of tiny white Christmas lights among the trees of Opryland. "Ain't this Opryland? Huh?"

After a few wrong turns we find a service road that takes us alongside Opryland to a place where the chain-link fence opens and a guard, bundled up and holding a clipboard, stands in the middle of the street under bright lights.

"Pull over here," Jimmy says. "Lower your window. Roll your *glass* down, now. Roll your glass on down. You need to talk to this guy right here. *Hold* it. . . ."

We pull up to the guy and I say hi and he says, "Hi, y'all," and bends down to look in my window, at which point Jimmy yells out *"HEY,"* in a happy greeting, and the guy says, "Hey, Mr. Martin!" cheerfully, and Jimmy, looking across me out my window, hollers back, *"Mister Martin? Mister?* Just say *Jimmy.* . . . I'm goin' rabbit huntin' tomorrow. . . ."

A woman comes over, another guard, also bundled up and carrying a clipboard; she approaches, hollers, "Hi, Jimmy. You

got you a driver now?" and Jimmy says, "Who is *this? Candy?*"
"Yes," she answers, coquettishly, and Martin says, "Candy . . .
I *love* you," "I love you too," she answers. Jimmy says, "Can we
just pull in over here some place?" and the guy says, "Just pull
in the dock, over on the other side of the van," and Candy says,
"Over on the other side of that van, there by the canopy in that
second dock," and Jimmy says, "Just where I can get out of
everybody's way," and they both smile and say, sure, go ahead,
and as we start pulling away, Martin hollers, "*LOVE* you
. . . *MERRY CHRISTMAS. . . .*" As we pull away I breathe
deeply in relief; they knew him, they were happy to see him,
he was on good terms with them, and I begin to think that the
evening might smooth out after all. A tall, rangy looking guy in
denim with a cowboy hat and carrying a guitar case is walking
in front of the limo, toward the entrance in front of us, and I
slow down a little. "I don't want to run over this guy with the
guitar, here," I say.

"*Fuck* 'im," Martin says.

I get the limo situated right next to a loading bay; before
we get out Martin finds the bottle of Knob Creek, which he
has been looking for, and we both take swigs, then get out and
head for the stage door.

Swarms of people mill around inside the brightly lit reception area, under the gaze of a security officer and a tough-looking middle-aged lady at the security desk; people are greeting each other, coming and going, musicians walking in with instrument cases, and the first impression is of a high school on the night of a big basketball game. The lady at the desk knows Jimmy and waves us in, and before ten seconds have gone by, he is saying "Hey! Willie!" to a short guy with short, salt-and-pepper hair and a well-trimmed moustache. His name is Willie Ackerman, a drummer who played on a number of Jimmy's recordings in the 1960s. "I put the bass drum in bluegrass music," he says. "Good to meet you," I say. We mill along together for a few moments in the crowd and he and Martin exchange some small talk.

I am at the Grand Ole Opry, backstage. It feels, indeed, like a big night at the high school, down to the putty-colored metal lockers that line the hall, the dressing rooms off the hall, with people crowding in and spilling out into the general stream—laughter, snatches of jokes and gossip overheard as you pass along—the halls even have the same dimensions of a high school hall, crowded with people, men and women, men with very dyed-looking hair and rhinestone-studded suits and guitars around their shoulders; at one point I recognize Charlie Louvin, of the Louvin Brothers. I follow Jimmy, who

With Bob Whittaker, former manager of the Grand Ole Opry.
Photograph by Jim Herrington

With Little Jimmy Dickens. *Photograph by Jim Herrington*

With Brent Burkett, of the Opry singing group the Four Guys, and Burkett's wife Jackie. *Photograph by Jim Herrington*

is alternately oblivious and glad-handing people as if he's running for senator. He attracts a fair amount of attention, even here, where flamboyance is part of the recipe.

Eventually we come to the dark, cave-like stage entrance, with heavy curtains going way up into the dark rigging above. The curtains at the front of the stage are closed, and I can hear the audience filing in out front. People in this area come and go with a more focused sense of purpose than out in the noisy halls; by the entrance to the area stand a guitarist and another young man and woman, harmonizing a bit. We walk into the bright, comfortable green room, just to the left of the stage entrance, and someone, a big man with stooped shoulders, comes over to Jimmy.

"Jimmy, how you doin' there?" he says, putting his arm around Martin and shaking his hand. "How's the old Hall of Fame member?"

"Well," Jimmy says, "I'm a Hall of Fame member, and the big booker ain't booked me *shit*."

Glancing at me a little embarrassedly, the other guy says, "Well, you never know; tomorrow's a brand-new day." We stand for a minute listening to the little group singing their song. "They're singing some bluegrass right over there," the man says. Martin grunts. This must be difficult for him being here, I think, like crashing a party. He seems to go in and out of his drunkenness; sometimes he's lucid, other times he has trouble putting a sentence together.

Now another man comes up and asks him, "Are you on the Opry tonight?"

Martin says, "No. They won't let me on it."

"Well, when are you going to get the hell on it?"

"Hey, Charlie," Martin says, grinning, "I can get out there and sing it and put it over!"

"I know it. I've seen you do it. Get out there and sing one."

Martin seems pleased by the encounter. He gets the two

men seated; he's going to tell them a joke. Two women are walking around a shopping mall, carrying heavy baskets full of all the stuff they bought. They get tired at one point and they sit down. After they've been sitting fifteen, twenty minutes, one of them says, "I tell you, I got to get up here; my rear end done plum went to sleep on me." The other one says, "I thought it did; I thought I heard it *snore* three or four times."

Great laughter at the joke. "Now you beat *that*, goddamn it," Martin says, triumphantly. We walk away, toward the stage area.

This is going okay, I think. He's seen some old friends, his ego's getting stroked, people seem to like having him around. Who knows?, I think. Maybe they will invite him to join after all.

We approach the small group that had been singing, and Jimmy stops. He says, "You're going to play on the Grand Ole Opry?"

"Yes, sir," the young man with the guitar says. He puts his hand out and says, "How are you doing, Mr. Martin?"

"What are you going to sing on it?" Jimmy asks.

"I'm playing with Ricky Skaggs," he says.

"Yeah?" Jimmy says.

"Yeah," the young man says. "Gonna play a little bluegrass tonight."

"A little bluegrass," Jimmy says.

"Yeah."

"Well," Jimmy begins, "he's about the *sorriest* fuckin' blue-grass you could ever hope to be on *with*, I'll tell you."

All three look at him, still smiling, but a little stunned; the woman says, "Ohhhh," as if he must be trying to make a good-humored joke that he has just taken a little too far, and the young man with the guitar, smiling more broadly, says, "Well, bless your heart. . . ."

"Well," Martin says, even louder now, "I'm just telling you, he's about the sorriest bluegrass, and *tell him I said it.*"

"I'll do it," the young man says, smiling even more broadly, as Martin lumbers off.

I start off after Martin, who abruptly stops, turns around, and adds, "*Hey*, bring him over here and let *me* tell him that."

"He's back there," the young man yells after us.

Now we're making our way along through the dark backstage area, and I'm thinking maybe I should just lead Martin out of here before something really bad happens. He's heading for another well-lit area, where some instruments—fiddles, banjos—are tuning up, sawing away, warming up. "Didn't I tell him?" Jimmy says to me, proudly. "Let's see if we can see anybody back here."

Now we enter a brightly lit, garage-like area, with musicians milling around, and a number of older men who look like a certain type you still see behind the scenes at prizefights— slit-eyed, white-shoed, pencil moustaches, sitting in chairs, watching everything. "Hello, Jimmy," someone says; a middle-aged man walking toward us, with a banjo, wearing a plaid sports shirt. "Good to see you, man," the man says, with genuine warmth. They shake hands. They make some small talk, mostly Jimmy talking about his hunting plans. The banjoist seems to know all about the hunting and the dogs. Then Jimmy tells him the joke about the two women. The banjoist laughs and laughs. "I don't want you to *steal* this on me, now," Jimmy says. Everything seems to be cool again.

Then Jimmy says, "Let's me, you, and Brewster do a tune." The banjoist calls the guitarist and singer Paul Brewster over. Across the room I see a big guy walk by, with a kind of combination crewcut and bouffant hairstyle, carrying a mandolin; it's Ricky Skaggs.

From my left side I suddenly hear Martin's voice, loud, hollering, "Is that the *BIGGEST ASSHOLE* in Nashville?"

Immediately the banjoist launches into a loud, unaccompanied solo, Earl Scruggs–style, an old Bill Monroe–Lester Flatt tune from the late 1940s called "Will You Be Loving Another Man?" and it is beautiful, ringing, pure and uncut, and, his attention distracted like a bull's by a red cape, Martin

begins singing the refrain, the banjoist and the guitarist joining in with the harmony, then Martin sings the first verse over
just the banjo, his voice piercing and brilliant, then the refrain
again, with the harmony, and the banjo comes in for a solo,
so spangling and stinging and precise, the melody appearing
out of a shower of rhythmic sequins and winking lights and
now Martin comes in for another chorus, with the banjo
underneath him telegraphing a constant commentary, goading
and dancing around Martin's melody, and it's as if they have
all levitated about six inches off the floor, pure exhilaration,
and by far the best music I have heard during my time in
Nashville.

When it's over there is that lag of a few seconds that it
always takes for reality to be sucked back into the vacuum
where great music has been, and as reality returns, along with
it strides Ricky Skaggs.

"Hey, Jimmy," he says, pleasantly, walking over to our little
group, strumming his mandolin, perhaps a little bit nervously.
"How you doin'?"

"Okay," Martin says, making it sound, somehow, like a
challenge. "How *you* doin'?"

"Okay." Strum, strum.

"Think you can still sing tenor to me?" Oh, no, I think.

Skaggs laughs, strums a little more. "I don't know. If you don't get it too high for me."

"Ricky, it's left up to you," Martin says. "It's not left up to me. If you want to make a ass out of yourself and don't want to sing tenor with me, don't do it. *He* can sing tenor with me . . . ," indicating Paul Brewster, who had been taking the high part in the song they had just sung.

"He sure can," Skaggs says, strumming, already regretting that he has come over. "He sings a good tenor to me."

"But *you* can't sing tenor to me," Martin persists. "You did with Ralph Stanley, didn't you?"

"I was sixteen then," Skaggs answers.

"He lost his balls, huh?" Martin says, to the few of us gathered around. "He lost his balls; he can't sing tenor with Jimmy no more."

Strum, strum.

"I can sing lead with any sumbitch who's ever sung . . . ," Martin says.

"You sure can," Skaggs says.

"Huh?"

"You sure can," Skaggs says, no longer looking at Martin.

Not to be placated, Martin goes on, "You let me down."

"I couldn't sing it that high, Jimmy."

"You didn't *hurt* me," Martin says, "about making money. I made it."

"That's right, you sure did," Skaggs says. Then, wearing a Mona Lisa smile and nodding politely, he says, "Good to see you guys," and steps away.

Skaggs and his band rehearse a few numbers, now, and Martin stands watching them, and they sound good, especially the banjoist and the lead guitar player, who is astounding. Jimmy stands listening, more or less unimpressed. At one point a short man in a white cowboy hat and blue cowboy suit comes over and it turns out to be Little Jimmy Dickens, one of the legends of the Opry, and the two of them stand there with an arm

Photograph by Jim Herrington

around each other's shoulder, watching Skaggs' band rehearse, and I'm glad Jimmy's found a port in the storm.

Now I kind of pull back and listen; I just want to enjoy being here a little bit. If Martin can survive being that much of a pain in the ass to someone, then he can probably weather just about anything. A while goes by, and then quicker movements begin to thread through the crowd, among the laughter and the picking, and someone calls out, "Five minutes till segment," and it's getting time for the Opry to start.

We move to the backstage area, the wings; the backup musicians are taking their places, and the backup singers are gathering around the mikes, the curtain is still closed, and the band hits a fast breakdown song, and before I know it the audience is visible, and cheering, and Porter Wagoner is leading things off, a gleaming white silhouette in front of the yawning cavern of the audience, a glowing nimbus around him and his bejeweled suit.

The first act on the bill is Little Jimmy Dickens himself, who hits the stage like a bomb going off, gyrating and singing "Take an Old Cold Tater And Wait," which has been his Opry signature tune since the 1950s; his guitar is almost as big as he is, and he shakes so much that he looks as if he's wrestling an alligator. After Dickens leaves the stage, to huge applause, Wagoner talks to the audience a little then introduces Skeeter Davis, who sings her old hit "The End of the World." During each tune, the upcoming performers gather behind the curtain just off to the side of the stage to watch the act preceding them.

Everybody does one song apiece, 80-year-old Bill Carlisle comes out and does an act combining singing and high-jumping, and it's a good variety show, but as I stand and watch I can't help thinking that it's almost as if Jimmy Martin would be too strong a flavor to introduce into this stew, like uncorking corn liquor at a polite wine tasting. The performers appear one by one, as if they are making cameo appearances in a movie about the Opry, and I can't see Martin fitting into it. Anyway, in his frustration he does everything he can to make sure he won't get on. He lashes out almost as if he's trying to give himself some sense that he's the one in control, that he's the one on the offensive, and not just sitting there helplessly. Whatever his reasons, he is doing exactly what he needs to do to keep himself off the Opry.

During Jimmy C. Newman's number, it occurs to me that Martin has been very quiet. He was talking to someone for a while, but now he is standing at the theater rope that demarks the small area of the wings where the performers are about to go on, and he has been standing there silently for quite a

Photograph by Jim Herrington

while. I look at him, and his gaze is fixed straight ahead, and I'm thinking something doesn't look right, maybe it is just the difficulty of watching the party going on around him, but I say, "Hey, Jimmy—everything okay?"

No answer; he keeps staring straight ahead.

"Jimmy—is everything alright?"

Now he turns his head just a little in my direction and squints as if to say, Hold on a minute, I'm thinking about something.

Then, nodding in the direction of a small group of people standing just offstage behind the curtain, he says, "Go over there and tell Bill Anderson to come over here. I'm going to knock his ass right off him."

"What are you talking about?" I say.

"Will you just go over there and tell him to come here and we can go outside—"

"I'm not going to do that," I say. "Hold on a second—hey," I say, trying to get his attention. "What happened?" This is not cool; Anderson is one of the Opry's biggest stars and has been since the mid-1960s. What this is about I have no idea.

"He talked to me in a way I don't like to be talked to, and I'm going to knock his ass off. I'll go over there *myself* . . . ," and he moves as if to climb over the theater cord, and I grab his arm and say, "Hold on, man, what are you doing? You don't want to do this. *Hey* . . . Jimmy . . ." People are starting to notice, now.

"I *will*," he says. "I'll knock him down right *here*—"

"Hold on, man," I say, under my breath, "You don't want to do this. Don't . . ." —and here I have an inspiration— " . . . don't *lower* yourself into that. The hell with Bill Anderson," I say, laying it on thick. "What does it matter what he says? Come on," I say, "let's get out of here, okay? I've seen enough. . . . I'm bushed. . . . Let's get out of here and have a drink. . . ."

It's too late, though; as I'm saying this, Bill Anderson walks past us with a couple of other men, not looking at us, heading toward the green room, and Martin lunges toward them. I step in front of him to hold him back, and as I do this I can tell that it is some kind of charade, because he doesn't struggle. As soon as the group passes Martin hollers out to the people who have been watching, "He walked right *by* me. . . . If he hadn't a-been holdin' me *back* I woulda knocked his *ass* off," and meanwhile someone out on stage is singing about yet another Lonely Heartbreak, and it occurs to me that it will be a miracle if they ever even let Jimmy Martin set foot backstage again at the Opry after this, much less perform. Calling someone an asshole is one thing, but moving on someone in front of witnesses is another. I've got to get him out of here, and I say to him now, "Come on, let's get the hell out of here, screw Bill Anderson anyway," and he kind of nods.

But before I can pull him away he stands for a long moment looking out toward the stage, and the singer and the audience. Impatient to get him out before something worse happens, I, who have come to the Opry very late in the game, say, "Come on, Jimmy, let's go." Then Jimmy Martin, who might well be taking his last look at the biggest dream of his life, turns around and walks out.

❧ ❧ ❧

I spent Saturday tooling around the city, buying CDs and souvenirs and just looking around, with the previous night looming in my mind like a weird nightmare. I called Martin in the afternoon; he had a hunting buddy over visiting him and he sounded rested and happy.

On Sunday morning I called again to say goodbye, and he volunteered to come down and meet me for breakfast at the Hardee's by the Holiday Inn. While I waited for him I tried to think if there was anything I wanted to ask him that I hadn't already asked him, but there wasn't.

He arrived late—car trouble, of course—in the limo, and we had breakfast. Martin ordered fried chicken. We talked for a few minutes about different things, but what was most on Martin's mind was a set of videotapes of stars of the Grand Ole Opry he saw advertised on television and which he thought I should get. "All of 'em is on there," he said, "Rod Brasfield, Minnie Pearl, Roy Acuff, Uncle Dave Macon," and on and on, and he talked about each one lovingly, especially Brasfield, a comedian whom Martin called "the best thing ever to hit Nashville." Martin wasn't making a nominating speech for himself this morning; he was just thinking about the people who made him want to do what he has been doing for almost fifty years, with an enthusiasm that reached back to the little shoeless kid's awe and love for those voices coming out of the radio. "Get 'em," he says, "if you wanna see the real thing. The *real* thing," he said, with lots of meaning in the emphasis.

Eventually it's time for me to go, and we head out into the bright morning. Before I go, though, he wants to tell me a joke. "There was this guy, said he could go around and talk to statues in town, and they'd talk back to him. So one day he walked up to this one, and, God, it was a big 'un, and he says, 'Old man statue, this is so-and-so.' The statue said, 'Yeah, glad to meet you.' So he says, 'Listen, what would be the first thing you would do if you could come alive for a hour?' And the statue answered him back, said, 'Shoot me *ten million pigeons*. . . .'" I don't know if he means this to be a little parable of our couple of days together—I doubt it—but it occurs to me that it works as such, and I laugh along with him.

Then Martin, in his blue jumpsuit, black nylon windbreaker, and dirty white mesh cap, gets into his limo, which starts up with a gurgling roar, and I watch and wave as he backs her out, wheels her around, and rides off into the distance up Old Hickory Boulevard in a midnight-blue blaze of country grandeur, the *KING OF BLUEGRASS* himself.

Afterword

When "True Adventures" was originally published in 1997, in the *Oxford American*'s first annual Southern Music issue, it seemed to strike some kind of nerve. I got mail and telephone calls from different parts of the country, much of it from musicians and others involved in the music business, telling me not just that they had enjoyed reading about Martin, but that something about him had moved them. I ran into people in Washington, D.C., Nashville, Lafayette, New York, and Memphis who had read and, to my amazement, practically memorized it, asking me questions about tiny details. It even turned out that certain musicians had been faxing the piece back and forth around the country.

Something about Martin got to other people, just as it got to me. I'm not entirely sure what it is. Although I've tried to boil it down, Martin resists any attempt at reduction. Maybe that is a beginning toward understanding him in the first place. But there are clues here and there.

After our conversation the first morning, on the way out through his wood-paneled den, we passed a wall arrangement of his album covers and I asked him which was his favorite.

With his forefinger he jabbed at the cover of *This World Is Not My Home*, his first gospel album for Decca, and said, "That one right there." A moment after saying this, Martin noticed something on the floor and bent to pick it up. It was a mousetrap with a recently deceased mouse in it. After examining it matter-of-factly for a few moments he discarded the mouse, but there was some cheese left in the trap, cheese you wouldn't have thought even a rat would eat. Jimmy handed me the blood-and-God-knows-what-else-encrusted trap, and the piece of cheese, and asked me to bait and set the trap again to catch another mouse. I don't know why he thought this was an appropriate thing to ask me to do, but I did it, with him watching me the whole time.

This is an entirely representative anecdote. Like many of the things Martin does, it seemed to involve a test. The implicit question, here, seemed to be: How willing are you to get your hands dirty?

In some ways Martin poses that same question to Nashville. Martin, I think, represents a reality that the New Nashville has tried to sanitize out of the picture. And yet he refuses to go away, in any sense. He is himself, unapologetically. In an era when so much of everything seems to consist of spin control, and public relations, and hidden agendas, Martin hides nothing, and he doesn't particularly care how you feel about it.

Nashville may change, but he will not. Martin has survived, like the occasional old building you see in a downtown somewhere, where the owner has refused to sell, and which stubbornly continues its own life amid the glossy skyscrapers. He has created room for himself. (Maybe that's overly romantic. It's entirely conceivable to me that Martin would sell, if he knew how. But he doesn't know how, and that fact has not broken him.)

Martin takes up space. Time, too, seems to change character around him. On the night we went to the Opry, for example, after his sartorial transformation at the beginning of the evening, after the trail of tears with the limo, after he told off the young bluegrass guitarist, after the encounter with Ricky Skaggs, after the near-disaster with Bill Anderson, after conversations with Skeeter Davis, who obviously had great affection for Jimmy, and Bill Carlisle, who seemed nervous around him, after steering him out through the backstage area and out past the lady at the desk and, eventually, back to the limo, which somehow started without difficulty for once, and after backing out of the parking bay without hitting anyone, and listening to Jimmy rant about Bill Anderson all the way back down Briley Parkway and back out east on I-40 to Hermitage, and up Old Hickory Boulevard, and then arriving at that long driveway, and maneuvering the limo back up to the top of the hill, back to where his dogs were waiting for him in the cold night air, I helped him out of the car, declined an invitation to spend the night at his house, and watched after him as he stumbled his way to the screen door and let himself in. Then I unlocked my car, climbed in, and locked the door, and I sat there in the dark, quiet at last, feeling as if steam were coming off of me. Finally, after thinking back a little on the whole, long, strange night, I put the key in the ignition and started the car, and out of the darkness of the dashboard in front of me the digital clock appeared, in electric blue letters, reading 8:30. It was only 8:30.

Even now, once I get cranked up talking about him it's hard to stop. Everyone who encounters him seems to have the same experience; everyone has a story. One senses they'll never stop, because Martin will never stop, although it looked close for a while late in 1997, when he had quadruple bypass surgery. Recuperating at home, he was visited by a musician who had worked with him from time to time. Edging up to the bed, the musician said, "Jimmy, you're gonna have to slow down on the drinking now; you had a quadruple bypass." And Martin, defiant, ever ready to show everyone that he's had it even worse than they think he has, shook his head, holding up four fingers. "Uh-uh," he said. *"Four."*

A month after his heart surgery, I received a phone call from a young woman who worked at the New Orleans Tower Records. After establishing that I was the Tom Piazza who had written the Jimmy Martin piece, she told me that a group of them at the store had read the piece and had heard about the heart attack in the papers. They wanted to send Jimmy a get-well card. Of course I gave them his address; I hope he got the card. I couldn't imagine a better coda to "True Adventures."

Except maybe for one. It would be great to see Martin become a member of the Opry; it has been his life's dream, as is clear from the piece. Who knows if it will happen? You see a man with so much talent, and who is, in so many ways, his own worst enemy. Yet his weakness, in this respect, is also his strength; he has never been digested by any of the homogenizing forces at work in Nashville. He will never—could never—turn into something other than what he is. The old guard at the Opry is a very small society, with a very defined hierarchy, one that has fought hard, in a number of ways, to be taken seriously, and Martin represents an untameable reality from which they have tried to distance themselves. So while one could hope that Martin gets his life's wish, one understands, too, what would make it difficult for him to get it. And what I wrote in the piece I still feel: it's almost as if he's too strong a taste for the Opry, as the Opry stands now. Still, it would be nice to think that a place could be made for him in country music's most venerable institution. Difficult or not, he is one of the masters, and he deserves it.

In any case, after all is said and done, the music is what

matters. Through all the ups and downs of his career Martin has never lost sight of that; he may have suffered, but his music has not. Whether Martin gets on the Opry or not, the sound of his voice and guitar will endure on some of the best bluegrass recordings ever made. They are the most important legacy of this unique, frustrating, contradictory, and deeply gifted man. What follows is a brief listing of some of the high spots of that legacy.

Photograph by Jim Herrington

The Recordings of Jimmy Martin

As of this writing, Jimmy Martin's recording career spans almost exactly fifty years, during which time he has amassed an extraordinary body of work, much of which hasn't yet received its proper due. This essay isn't an attempt at a full-scale assessment of Martin's recorded work. Rather, it is a personal tour of what I consider to be the high points.

Martin's first recordings were done with Bill Monroe's Blue Grass Boys, for Decca, beginning in February 1950. Although he left Monroe for a time and recorded with Bobby Osborne on King, he returned to the Blue Grass Boys and recorded with Monroe through January 1954. From the first, Martin added an unprecedented intensity to the band. Instrumentally, his guitar propelled the rhythm with strong, aggressive bass runs. But equally important was Martin's singing ability. In Martin, the strong-willed, idiosyncratic Monroe found an equal who could match his own vocal precision and nuance, and their voices combined to produce some of the finest duet performances in bluegrass.

Their first duet record, from February 1950, "Memories

Photograph by Jim Herrington

of You," has Martin rock-solid under Monroe's high tenor, generating an eerie beauty. A later session that day produced the fine "I'm Blue, I'm Lonesome," with Martin and Monroe bending notes together, hand in glove; they had grown very close very quickly. "Boat of Love," recorded two months later, is a gospel quartet number on which Martin's lead is distinctive; listen to the way he phrases "Don't wait too late / to make your reservation . . ." —he swings.

In October 1950 they recorded the Monroe standard "Uncle Pen," on which Martin contributed a forceful ascending "G run" in the guitar's bass strings. While that moment is justly celebrated, Martin's powerful guitar conception animates almost all of these recordings. The same session produced the classic "River of Death," where Martin sings a beautiful lead, lining out the song for the rest of the quartet. His voice already has its beautiful nasal quality, although it is still mellow compared to how it would sound a few years later. A January 1951 session produced the pure power and raw beauty of "Letter From My Darlin'," a quintessential heartbreak song, on which the Monroe/Martin vocal blend and phrasing are perfect. (At his 1995 induction into the IBMA Hall of Honor, Martin announced that no one could beat him and Bill Monroe singing bluegrass, and this is an example of why.) The same 1951 session also produced "On The Old Kentucky Shore," which is almost as good as "Letter from My Darlin'"; listen for the detailing in the bent notes.

July 18, 1952, was a red-letter day for the band; in two sessions Martin recorded some of his best tracks with Monroe. Among them is a terrific version of "In The Pines," with a haunting wordless falsetto section; listen, too, to Martin's fine, pushing guitar work behind Monroe's mandolin break. Country music historian Charles Wolfe rightly calls "Memories of Mother and Dad" one of their best duets, with its razor-sharp harmony, neck-and-neck even on the unusual flourishes and trail-offs at the ends of lines. Also great is "The Little Girl and the Dreadful Snake." Martin's guitar work is worth a special listen on the duet "My Dying Bed." Other standouts from their later work together include "I Hope You Have Learned" (November 1953) with Monroe and Martin in full cry, and "Sitting Alone In the Moonlight," from January 1954.

All of the above mentioned tracks are available on *Bill Monroe: Bluegrass 1950–1958*, a four-CD set from Bear Family Records (BCD 15423), which anyone interested in bluegrass music needs to own. A number of them—including "I'm Blue, I'm Lonesome," "In The Pines," and "Memories of Mother and Dad"—are also available on MCA's fine four-disc collection *The Music of Bill Monroe from 1936 to 1994* (MCAD4 11048), which also contains very illuminating notes by John Rumble of the Country Music Foundation.

Martin left Monroe for good in 1954 and teamed up with the young Bobby and Sonny Osborne. With them, he recorded a November 1954 session for RCA that is most notable for the classic original version of "20/20 Vision." Over a brisk waltz tempo, Martin sings Joe Allison and Milton Estes' clever, stinging lyrics about a man deceived and devastated by a cheating lover ("This is my punishment / death is too kind / 20/20 vision / and walkin' 'round blind"). It remains one of Martin's most famous recordings.

But Martin really came into his own when he started recording under his own name for Decca in 1956. The association with Decca, which lasted until 1974, produced a huge amount of enduring music. Readers who have a taste for Jimmy Martin's music are encouraged to buy the five-CD boxed set put out by Bear Family (*Jimmy Martin and the Sunny Mountain Boys*, Bear Family BCD 15705 EI); it includes all of Martin's Decca recordings, along with the RCA tracks with the Osborne Brothers. The enclosed booklet contains a biography, lots of rare photos, clippings, and other memorabilia. It also contains a complete discography and a detailed, comprehensive session-by-session essay on the recordings, written by historian Chris Skinker, which includes plenty of anecdotes about the events around the sessions. What I have done here is to try to point you to my personal favorites among this avalanche of material, things that I consider to be Martin high points.

His two 1956 Decca sessions produced the fine "Before the Sun Goes Down" and Martin's first version of "Grand Ole Opry Song," as well as "Hit Parade of Love," which became a regional hit. But in February 1958 Martin made the first of his records with the group, one that remains his favorite to this day, with Paul Williams on mandolin and high tenor vocal and the prodigy J. D. Crowe on banjo. Crowe would record steadily with Martin through August 1960, Paul Williams through August 1962. They would never surpass their first session, though; Martin was in full command of his vocal powers, alternating solo verses with tightly harmonized passages with Crowe and Williams. The instrumental chemistry was also bracing to say the least; listen to Martin's guitar runs against Crowe's banjo on "Sophronie," for just one example. "Ocean of Diamonds" was a big hit and an early masterpiece of the group, as was "I'll Never Take No For an Answer." They also recorded a couple of tracks with religious themes that day, including "Voice Of My Savior," which show that Martin could put as much fire into his religious performances as he did into his secular ones. It's probably fair to call this one of the best single recording sessions in bluegrass history.

Their next session, in November 1958, produced the tear-jerker "She's Left Me Again," a very strong Martin performance, as well as "Hold Whatcha Got," a perennially popular Martin song, co-written by Williams and Martin. "Wooden Shoes," from January 1960, is a sappy song that gets better treatment than it deserves from Martin, his clear, nasal tones ringing through with just a nice trace of grit in there for traction. The theme of the lyrics (a love left behind in a foreign land, a big theme in the wake of World War II) is similar to that of the well-known "Fraulein," which Martin recorded six years later almost to the day and which is one of his greatest performances. In 1960 Martin also made his first recording of Jimmie Skinner's "You Don't Know My Mind," a tune which he would revisit from time to time throughout his career, and turned in a fine performance of an original weeper called "Don't Cry To Me." In August he recorded another solid heartbreak song, "Undo What's Been Done." The August 1960 session would be the last one for J. D. Crowe during his first tenure with Martin, although the banjoist would come back to the studio with Martin from time to time over the next few years.

One fugitive recording from this period not included on

the Bear Family boxed set was issued as *Big Jam Session* (available on cassette as Old Homestead OHCS-159). It contains a spoken introduction by Martin indicating that it was taped in Texas at the home of some fans. On it, Martin, Crowe, and Williams tackle a number of bluegrass standards not recorded by them for Decca, including "Molly and Tenbrooks," "Angel Band," and "Roll In My Sweet Baby's Arms." There's also a fun version of "Gotta Travel On." The sound quality isn't great, but it's not terrible, and this captures the Crowe/Williams edition of the Sunny Mountain Boys at its most relaxed.

Back at the Decca studios, an October 1961 double session produced another good performance of a Jimmie Skinner song, "Don't Give Your Heart To A Rambler," which had more or less the same message as the previous year's "You Don't Know My Mind." Also from that session came "God Guide Our Leader's Hand." Released in April 1962, between the Berlin crisis and the Cuban missile crisis, the song is a warning against "a war with these mighty destructive weapons," containing a harrowing image of nuclear destruction and ending by saying "we should pray for a great worldwide revival / Instead of trying to see who's the strongest man." At the same session Martin recorded the lonesome train song "Mr. Engineer," which features an airborne duet with Paul Williams, and another sacred duet on "This World Is Not My Home."

Two sessions in August 1962 produced eleven very strong gospel songs and set another high-water mark for Martin. The combination of Martin's voice with Paul Williams' tenor is almost overwhelmingly powerful in spots, notably on "Give Me Your Hand" and the traditional "What Would You Give In Exchange for Your Soul." And "Stormy Waters," on which Williams sings a piercing, high, and unforgettable lead over a churning waltz background, is a bona fide masterpiece. These three tracks, especially, are among Martin's very greatest, but almost everything from these two sessions is outstanding. In late 1963 Martin recorded "Widow Maker," the story of a truck-driving tragedy, which became a big hit. He also turned in a kicking performance of "I'm Thinking Tonight of My Blue Eyes." (J. D. Crowe, back with Martin briefly, plays a tasty solo on this.)

Martin had truly hit his stride, and he made some of his most fully realized recordings in 1964 and 1965. A February 1964 session produced excellent versions of "There's More Pretty Girls Than One" and the Dave Dudley hit "Six Days On The Road" (following up on the truck drivers' theme he had addressed with "Widow Maker"). The session also produced "Truck Driver's Queen," which is nowhere near as cheesy as the title might suggest and which earns a solid vocal from Martin, and "Truck Driving Man." In August another outstanding session produced one of his best tearjerkers, "It Takes One To Know One," in which Martin really cranks up the emotional juice, as well as his hit "Sunny Side of the Mountain," a pumping, exhilarating performance. Also recorded that day was the under-recognized "Snow White Grave," a subtle vocal tour de force for Martin, full of his characteristic vocal breaks and flourishes, as well as the novelty tune "Guitar Picking President."

An equally good session in March 1965 produced great Martin vocals in "Poor Ellen Smith," "Shenandoah Waltz," and Charlie Monroe's "I'm Comin' Back But I Don't Know When." Later that year brought his unusual "The Last Song," a kind of retirement threat, which came out of a session that also produced some powerhouse instrumentals, including "Theme Time."

By this point Martin's voice had taken on a depth and power that put him in a class of his own. Underneath that power was a subtlety and command of the details of the style that unquestionably marked him as a master. All these 1964 and 1965 recordings show Martin at the top of his game, at a level he would maintain for a long time. One of his very greatest recordings is "Fraulein," recorded at another hot session in January of 1966. Martin's performance on "Fraulein," Lawton Williams' ode to a love left behind overseas, is so good, so subtle, that it may not hit you all at once the first time you hear it. The pure beauty of the sound of his voice at this point is really something to hear, but even better is what he does with it. Pay special attention to the way Martin makes little turns at the ends of lines, lets his voice break just enough to be expressive but not enough to be bathetic. Listen, in just the first line, to what he does with the words "blue," "waters," and "Rhine." It all sounds so natural and expressive that you might forget that it is the result of conscious choice and training.

Also recorded at that session were Bill Monroe's "The Summer's Come and Gone," with Jimmy nailing that high and lonesome sound, as he does on Hank Williams' "You're Gonna Change (Or I'm Gonna Leave)." "Tennessee Waltz" is another performance in which Martin subtly but unmistakably makes a familiar tune his own.

"Living Like A Fool," from 1967, is one more of his good "she-left-me" performances, but it is only a warm-up for the great "Steal Away Somewhere and Die," from later in the year, one of the best performances of his career. This one takes it about as close to the edge as you want to get, but there is nothing faked or overwrought; Jimmy looks at the void of hopelessness in the wake of lost love and doesn't blink. Listen to the way he sings "And now there's nothing left but burning memories" in the last verse. "Losing You," a Martin original from 1968, is yet another of his best performances, and it has one of the great opening lines of all time. ("There's no such thing as sleep for jealous fools. . . .") Good as this version is, he would top it three years later on the Nitty Gritty Dirt Band's *Will The Circle Be Unbroken* album.

During the Decca years, Martin recorded many novelty tunes, such as "I Can't Quit Cigarettes," "Guitar Picking President," "Moonshine Hollow," and "Poor Little Bull Frog." These kinds of tunes have a central place in Martin's repertoire, as his coon-hunting songs would have in subsequent decades, but they are not my favorite part of his work. If I seem to give them less attention than other types of songs, it's just my personal preference at work.

Among Martin's good later Deccas is "Lonesome Prison Blues," a very solid performance in which Martin essentially shifts the locale of Bill Monroe's "Roane County Prison," to his own hometown, Sneedville. "When My Savior Reached Down For Me" is a beautiful gospel vocal. "I've Got My Future On Ice" is vintage Jimmy Martin in his blackest heartbreak mode; his voice breaks into a rueful, stifled laugh at the end of certain lines, which gives the performance a chilling effect. Terrific stuff.

"I'd Like To Be Sixteen Again" and "I Cried Again" come from a hot session with an excellent band including mandolinist Doyle Lawson, banjoist Alan Munde, and fiddler Kenny Baker. Martin's very last Decca session was notable for a strong performance of Hylo Brown's unusual "Lost To A Stranger."

The original Decca albums are technically out of print, but CD and cassette versions of some of them are available from the Ernest Tubb Record Shop and from Martin himself (addresses appear below). *Sunny Side of the Mountain* is probably the best of them, with the title song as well as "It Takes One To Know One," "I'm Comin' Back But I Don't Know When," "Snow White Grave," and "In The Pines." *Widow Maker* is not far behind, with "Six Days on The Road," "I'll Never Take No For An Answer," "There's More Pretty Girls Than One," and "Ocean of Diamonds." *Good & Country* has "You Don't Know My Mind," "Grand Ole Opry Song," "Hold Whatcha Got," and "All The Good Times Are Past & Gone." *I'd Like To Be Sixteen Again* is worth having for "I've Got My Future On Ice," "Lonesome Prison Blues," and the original "Losing You." *This World Is Not My Home*, a gospel set that Martin pointed out to me as his favorite of his own recordings, includes "Prayer Bell of Heaven" and the great "Give Me Your Hand."

While he was still under contract to Decca, Martin went into the studio with the Nitty Gritty Dirt Band in 1971 and recorded several tracks that appeared on *Will The Circle Be Unbroken*. Martin's performances of "Grand Ole Opry

Song," "Losing You," "Sunny Side of the Mountain," "Walking Shoes," and "You Don't Know My Mind" are phenom-
enal, in almost every case topping his original recordings of the
tunes. The first thing you hear on the record is Jimmy messing
with banjoist John McEuen—"Pick the banjo solid, John.
You picked one for fifteen years, didn't you?" Then it's off to
the races. On *Will the Circle Be Unbroken, Vol. 2*, released in
1989, Martin appears on one track, "I'm Sittin' On Top Of
The World," on which he sings well, but the backing is a little
automatic-sounding.

After leaving Decca, Martin recorded for the better part
of twenty years for the various labels associated with King
Records, and the material has come out in many forms and
on many small labels such as Hollywood, Gusto, Richmond,
and Deluxe, all of which swap around the same tracks. I will
concentrate here on material that should be easy to find as of
this writing.

An essential Martin item is *Jimmy Martin's 20 Greatest
Hits* (Deluxe DCD-7863). It contains a number of remakes,
in most cases even more spirited than the Decca originals,
including "Freeborn Man," "Truck Driving Man," "You Don't
Know My Mind," and "Widow Maker." It also includes a stun-
ning performance of "Don't Let Your Sweet Love Die," which

ranks with the Decca "Fraulein" as one of Martin's greatest vocals; very good versions of his later favorites "Lover's Lane" and "One Woman Man"; the surging novelty number "Bluegrass Singing Man" ("I got fifteen acres down in Moonshine Holler / When the creek runs dry we can't make a dollar"); and a searing version of the old-timer "Knoxville Girl." It also includes two tributes to Martin's favorite hunting dog of the time ("Pete, The Best Coon Dog In The State of Tennessee" and "Run, Pete, Run"). All in all, this is a perfect introduction to Martin.

One Woman Man (Hollywood HCD-440) is a good budget-priced collection; even with only ten cuts it is well worth picking up. One of the standouts here is his terrific performance of the heartbreak tune "I Can't Give My Heart Again"; listen to the way his voice breaks on the word "linger" in the first verse. Also fine are his treatments of two songs associated with Lester Flatt, "Will You Be Loving Another Man?" and "Down The Road." *King of Bluegrass* (Power Pak PKCD 10513) is a chintzy budget disc with only eight tracks, all but one of which are recycled from *One Woman Man* and *20 Greatest Hits*. But that one track makes the disc worth picking up, a romping version of the old Bill Monroe favorite "Goodbye Old Pal," a valedictory to a cowboy's horse; at the end of each verse Martin yodels for all he's worth, and the last yodel will knock a hole in your wall. You really need to hear this. *Jimmy Martin & Ralph Stanley: First Time Together* (Hollywood HCD-175) is another standout. Listen to Martin exhort Stanley to "play it like I taught you" during his banjo solo on "I'm Going Down the Road." Their voices blend well on favorites like "In The Pines" and "Roll On, Buddy, Roll On." "God Gave You To Me" is another especially fine performance here. A note: "Don't Let Your Sweet Love Die" was evidently included as filler; Stanley doesn't appear on this track.

Got It Made In The Shade . . . if a tree don't fall (SMR-006-CD), which Martin brought out himself in 1996, is a strong disc, notable especially for the title cut, a wry Martin original that conveys his personality well through some self-deprecating gallows humor. There are also versions of "Don't Let Me Cross Over," a duet with Little Jimmy Dickens, and Bill Monroe's "Rose of Old Kentucky," on which Martin is joined by his friend Marty Stuart. Martin also does a fine job on "Cora Is Gone," which is called "Darlin' Cory" here; this is the track that occasioned his disagreement with Ricky Skaggs at the Opry. Skaggs—who declined to sing the high tenor part Martin wanted him to sing—contributes one vocal verse and a cogent mandolin solo. The disc can be ordered directly from Martin or from the Ernest Tubb Record Shop.

Two recent live recordings are worth having for Martin's

monologues if nothing else. *Live in 1990 With Grant Turner* (Sunny Mountain Music SMM7882) is the better of the two musically. Introducing "It Takes One To Know One," Martin says, "It's a sad, crying song, a heartbreakin' song, and the way we sing it, it's a lot sadder. . . ." Introducing fiddler Vernon Derrick, Martin says, "He played with Hank Williams Jr. for seven years, and I guess Hank fired him and he come with me. . . ." *Live At The Ryman* (SMR 010), while undated, is obviously later and notable mainly for some prickly, eccentric monologues, again containing some vintage Martin moments. Pointing out a couple of local judges in the audience, Martin remarks, "I never have been wrong in any court I've been in yet, only when I got a divorce. [Laughs, hoots from audience.] Every musician that's listenin' to my voice, whatever you do, if you say 'I do,' be sure you got some kind of a little house to give her to sign the divorce papers."

As of right now there are four videos of Martin available. *Twenty-Five Year Reunion* (Bluegrass Classic Video) is a film of a 1987 Ohio festival reunion between Martin and J. D. Crowe and Paul Williams. The production qualities are not the highest in any respect, and the music is a bit on the unrehearsed-sounding side, but there are some very good moments here. *Induction to The I.B.M.A. Hall of Honor*, which Martin evidently put out himself, is an amateur video of the

1995 awards ceremony and subsequent jam session celebrating Martin's recognition by the International Bluegrass Music Association. This is a must for any connoisseur of Martin as a public figure. Once he is introduced and gets hold of the microphone to give his acceptance speech he won't let go, and his monologue is a classic mixture of humor, self-pity, self-promotion, and love for bluegrass music. *Live TV Show* contains a somewhat subdued recent television appearance in which Martin and the Sunny Mountain Boys perform several tunes, as well as some footage of Martin on a coon-hunting trip with a group of friends.

But the one to get, if you can find it, is the surreal classic *Jimmy Martin at His Home in Hermitage, Tennessee* (Grand Video 1001). After an introduction by Martin, this contains a series of homemade music videos in which Martin lip-synchs the lyrics to songs like "Widow Maker," "You Don't Know My Mind," and "Sunny Side of the Mountain" at various places around his home. It features cameo appearances by his then-wife Teresa and his daughter Lisa Sarah Martin, who joins her father, on the couch in the den, for a tearful duet of "Daddy, Will Santa Claus Ever Have To Die?"

The videos—along with the above-mentioned live tapes, *Got It Made In The Shade*, the CD and cassette versions of the Decca albums, as well as "King of Bluegrass" caps and various other items—can be ordered from the man himself, at Jimmy Martin Enterprises, P.O. Box 646, Hermitage, TN 37076. The phone number is (615) 883-0334.

The Ernest Tubb Record Shops also handle most of this material; they can be reached at P.O. Box 5000, Nashville, TN 37202-0500; phone 1-800-229-4288.

Highlights of
Jimmy Martin's Career

Compiled by JOHN RUMBLE
Historian, Country Music Foundation

with the research assistance of
PETE KUYKENDALL, NEIL ROSENBERG,
CHRIS SKINKER, *and* ROBERT GENTRY

Although no comprehensive biography has ever been attempted,
the outlines of Jimmy Martin's life and career are fairly clear.
The following chronology may provide background for under-
standing the events and character captured in True Adventures
with the King of Bluegrass.

1927: One of seven children born to Sara Burchette and Ease
Martin, James Henry Martin is born on August 10 in the East
Tennessee farming community of Sneedville.

1931–1948: After his father dies, when Jimmy is four, Jimmy has
a tough time relating to his stepfather, a stern disciplinarian.

Bill Monroe and Jimmy Martin onstage, circa late 1960s. *Archives of the Country Music Foundation*

The search for an understanding father figure will profoundly affect Jimmy's complex relationship with his idol, bluegrass pioneer Bill Monroe.

Martin is "raised up hard," working on his family's farm and hiring out to other local farmers. Saving $7.50 to buy a Sears, Roebuck Gene Autry–model guitar, he entertains family and friends with his energetic singing and playing.

Increasing conflicts with his stepfather prompt Martin to drop out of school around the eighth grade and move to Kingsport, Tennessee, to live with aunts. He works on local radio and in a Coca-Cola plant but is fired from the plant for singing on the job.

1949: By mid-year, Martin has moved to Morristown, Tennessee, where he works as a painter and performs with Tex Climer and the Blue Band Coffee Boys on radio station WCRK.

Late in the fall, Martin treks to Nashville and successfully auditions for *Grand Ole Opry* star Bill Monroe, who hires him after he draws encores at a Monroe appearance in Arkansas.

1950–1951: On February 3, 1950, in Nashville, Martin makes his first recordings for Decca Records as a member of Monroe's Blue Grass Boys. Over the next fourteen months, the band records classics like "My Little Georgia Rose," "I'm Blue, I'm

Charlie Cline, Bill Monroe, and Jimmy Martin in a publicity photo from the early 1950s. *Archives of the Country Music Foundation*

Lonesome," "Uncle Pen," and "Lord Protect My Soul" for the label. Martin's muscular rhythm guitar playing, powerful lead voice, and ability to blend vocally with Monroe spur Monroe to reshape his sound in the face of competition from Flatt and Scruggs and other newly emerging bluegrass groups.

1951–1952: Early in 1951, poor pay leads Martin to leave Monroe and join Ezra Cline's Lonesome Pine Fiddlers and singer-mandolinist Bobby Osborne for radio programs and personal appearances out of Bluefield, West Virginia.

On August 27, 1951, Martin and Osborne cut four sides for Cincinnati-based King Records, a leading independent label of the day. Sides include "My Lonely Heart" and "She's Just a Cute Thing." Record labels identify the act as Jimmy Martin, Bob Osborne, and the Sunny Mountain Boys, and Martin will retain the Sunny Mountain Boys name from this point on.

Martin, Osborne, and other musicians move to WCYB in Bristol, Virginia, but the band breaks up after finding it impossible to earn enough money on show dates to survive.

By early 1952, Martin and his newly constituted band are working Knoxville radio stations WROL and WNOX.

Around June of 1952, Martin moves to radio station WPFB in Middletown, Ohio, where he meets Bobby Osborne's younger brother Sonny, a budding banjo picker still in his teens.

1952–1954: By July 1952, Martin rejoins Bill Monroe's band. Among the numbers the band records between July 18, 1952, and January 25, 1954, are Monroe standards such as "In the Pines," "Memories of Mother and Dad," "On and On," and "Sitting Alone in the Moonlight."

1954–1955: Upset by Monroe's refusal to feature Martin's name on the labels of Monroe's records and sensing interest by other labels to record him in his own right, Martin leaves Monroe by the spring of 1954 and returns to WPFB in Middletown, Ohio.

In August 1954, together with Bobby and Sonny Osborne, Martin heads for Detroit, where they perform on radio station WJR's *Lazy Ranch Jamboree* and *Goodwill Jamboree*. In addition, they appear on CKLW-TV in nearby Windsor, Ontario, and on daily radio programs aired by radio station WEXL in Royal Oak, Michigan. The act tours Michigan and Ohio, sometimes playing shows with *Grand Ole Opry* stars.

Assisted by fiddler Red Taylor and bassist Cedric Rainwater, Martin and the Osbornes record six excellent sides for RCA in Nashville on November 16, 1954. Numbers include "Chalk Up Another One," "20/20 Vision," and "Save It! Save It!"

Martin and the Osbornes part ways in 1955, and over the next two years Martin continues broadcasting over Detroit-area stations with other band members, including mandolinist Earl Taylor and banjoist Sam "Porky" Hutchins.

1956: At a May 9 session held in Nashville's Bradley Studios, Martin records his first sides as a featured artist on Decca, with support from Taylor, Hutchins, Rainwater, and fiddler Tommy Vaden. "Hit Parade of Love" from this session is released in November and attracts attention in regional markets.

On December 1, Martin records four sides in Nashville, including "The Grand Ole Opry Song." Joining him are Taylor, Rainwater, fiddler Gordon Terry, and, for the first time in the studio, banjoist J. D. Crowe. Coached extensively by his boss, Crowe develops a distinctive style that helps to define Martin's sound.

1958–1959: On February 15, 1958, Martin's performance on the *Louisiana Hayride* barn dance program, broadcast on Saturday nights over the regionally powerful radio station KWKH in Shreveport, earns him a place in the cast. With other stars of this show, Martin tours in Texas, Arkansas, and the Southeast.

At a Nashville session held on February 19, 1958, Martin records six sides, including "Ocean of Diamonds" and "Sophronie," both standards of his repertoire. "Rock Hearts," also cut at this session, becomes Martin's first recording to reach *Billboard* magazine's country charts. Breaking the following December 8, it peaks at #14 within its six-week chart run.

1960–1962: By early 1960, Martin leaves the *Louisiana Hayride* and moves to the WWVA *World's Original Jamboree* radio barn dance in Wheeling, West Virginia. The show's strategic location gives him valuable exposure and allows him to tour widely with an enlarged band, especially in Pennsylvania and points north.

On May 16, 1960, Decca releases Martin's first album, *Good 'N Country*. Tracks include songs recorded from May 1956 through January 1960, such as "The Grand Ole Opry Song," "Hold Whatcha Got," "You Don't Know My Mind," and "I Like to Hear 'Em Preach It."

From August 1960 to August 1962, Martin records such memorable tunes as "My Walking Shoes Don't Fit Me Anymore," "Don't Give Your Heart to a Rambler," and "Tennessee."

Martin moves to Nashville in December 1962, in hopes of joining the *Grand Ole Opry*.

1963–1971: Working with prominent Nashville bookers like Hubert Long and Buddy Lee, Martin plays shows with top country acts such as Ferlin Husky, Merle Haggard, and Hank Williams Jr. But despite Martin's *Opry* guest appearances, management does not make him a regular.

In September 1965, Martin appears at Carlton Haney's first big bluegrass festival, in Fincastle, Virginia. This event heralds the growth of the bluegrass festival circuit, on which Martin becomes a mainstay.

Jimmy Martin and the Sunny Mountain Boys, (*left to right*) Paul Williams, J. D. Crowe, and Johnny Dacus, in a publicity photo for the WWVA Jamboree. *Archives of the Country Music Foundation*

During these years, Martin cuts important sides for Decca, including "Widow Maker" (a #19 hit of 1964), "Sunny Side of the Mountain," "Freeborn Man," "(I've Got My) Future on Ice," and "Milwaukee Here I Come."

1972–1973: In 1972, United Artists releases the landmark *Will the Circle Be Unbroken* album, a three-LP set featuring the Nitty Gritty Dirt Band in combination with Martin and fellow country musicians Earl Scruggs, Mother Maybelle Carter, Roy Acuff, Merle Travis, and Doc Watson. Five tracks showcase Martin: "The Grand Ole Opry Song," "Sunny Side of the Mountain," "You Don't Know My Mind," "Losing You (Might Be the Best Thing Yet)," and "My Walking Shoes Don't Fit Me Anymore." This strong-selling album widens country music's audience, especially among college-aged listeners.

Released as a single from *Will the Circle Be Unbroken*, "The Grand Ole Opry Song" reaches the lower levels of *Billboard*'s country charts in the summer of 1973.

1974: On April 10, Martin records his final session for MCA, which had earlier retired its Decca label for the time being. Martin then switches to the Gusto label for several years.

1989: MCA releases *Will the Circle Be Unbroken, Vol. 2*, featuring Martin's performance of "Sitting on Top of the World."

Jimmy Martin and his band, circa early 1970s. *Archives of the Country Music Foundation*

1990: Rounder Records, a leading independent label, especially famous for its reissue albums, releases *You Don't Know My Mind*, an album compiling vintage Martin recordings made between 1956 and 1966.

1994: German-based Bear Family Records issues a five-CD set containing Martin's complete Decca/MCA recordings.

1995: Martin is inducted into the International Bluegrass Music Association's Hall of Honor.

1999: The Country Music Foundation Press and Vanderbilt University Press publish Tom Piazza's *True Adventures with the King of Bluegrass*, which originally appeared in the *Oxford American*.

2001: *The King of Bluegrass*, an eighteen-song CD compiled by the Country Music Hall of Fame and Museum, appears on Audium.

2003: Producer and director George Goehl completes the documentary film *King of Bluegrass: The Life and Times of Jimmy Martin*.

2005: On May 14, Martin succumbs to bladder cancer and congestive heart failure. He is buried in Spring Hill Cemetery in Madison, a Nashville suburb.